# A Walk with My Father

Tahisha Hamed

# A Walk with My Father

## Tahisha Hamed

Destiny House Publishing

Detroit, MI

A Walk with My Father

Published by Destiny House Publishing, LLC

Copyright ©2013 October  Tahisha Hamed

ISBN: 978-1936867172

Printed in the United States of America

For information:

Destiny House Publishing, LLC

www.destinyhousepublishing.com

email: inquiry@destinyhousepublishing.com

P.O. Box 19774- Detroit, MI 48219 - 888-890-9455

# Table of Contents

# Introduction

This novel is my truth; my truth of my journey with God from 15-19 years of age. I'm taking readers on a journey of my emotions, thoughts, feelings, as they see how I transitioned from a faithless believer to a faithful believer. I wanted to share how I overcame from a teen to a young adult with having emotions & thoughts with no spiritual direction to one who has gained knowledge and growth from life & spiritual experiences. My purpose in writing this book is to show that this relationship with God is a process; just like a baby, this walk takes time to develop. To develop into that man/woman God calls you to be. I pray my story helps change many lives for the better and bring them closer to God.

-Tahisha Hamed

I CAN DO ALL THINGS THROUGH
CHRIST WHO STRENGTHENS ME!!!
**Philippians 4: 13**

# *The Beginning*
# *2005-2006 "Crawling"*

### *"Choices"*

We all make choices in life, where we hope that no

matter what happens the choice we made will help.

Sometimes that's true and sometimes it isn't. Most

people want everything in life to go perfect, and

they pray that everything does, but when things

don't go right they think their life is over. The

reason for that is because they don't know how to

make choices correctly and when you don't know

how to make choices correctly, you get confused.

When people make choices, they think they're

doing it for their best ability, but what happens

when your choice leads you down the wrong road of life? What are you to do then?

## 06/4/2005
Tonight was a wonderful night; I went to Youth Explosion and had a ball. Teenagers from different churches came also, and a few of these teens touched me very deeply and I began to cry. Towards the end a Rev made me laugh and I felt very good. I did a lot of thinking while I was there, made some decisions too. I watched how the young guys had that wonderful feeling inside while they performed and I wanted that feeling. It was like they didn't have any issues going on, and I said to myself, "Man if I had that feeling that they feel right now, all this pain I feel inside could just go away." I decided tonight is going to be the

night I finally talk to the Lord and tell Him what's on my mind and what my plans are with Him. I am so happy right now. Even though two people tried to bring negative energy to me, I dropped it and "Stood Up" like Mount Calvary Praise Team said tonight. Well I can only pray that things get better. Peace, Love, & Happiness –BELIEVE IN GOD!!!

**06/12/2005**
Today is Sunday; the day I always go to the Lord's house. But I guess I'm not. Do you know that person called me? The only reason they did that was to see if I was leaving and playing music. But it's okay because I have my cd player, cd's, and my Bible; so even if you try to keep me away from His house I still have Him with me. I really wish that person wouldn't do that because they know

how much I love church.  They told me how they

really felt about church and me last Sunday.

However, since I'm here and you don't agree with

me going I'll just read my Bible and receive

scriptures and sermon notes from other people.

The Lord knows I want to come to Him, but He

sees my situation so I know and pray He

understands and even though I'm not there Lord,

you are in my heart and I'll be coming to you

soon; don't know when but soon so soon I may not

be able to speak. BELIEVE IN GOD!!

# ***The Angel that Fell***

*Once there was this angel whom the Lord has*

*chosen to make the world a better place; she had*

*wanted to know; of all the angels why her? For she*

*loved everyone in a way the others hadn't or*

*couldn't; so she packed her bags and was ready to*

*take off; once she landed to earth, she had a*

*wonderful feeling inside; she traveled around the*

*world, putting love in their hearts, and showing*

*them a new way of making it to those gates of*

*Heaven; she had finally reached her last*

*destination; inside this city, in this home, was a*

*feeling the angel had never expected; of all the*

*ones whom she'd loved and taught them how to*

*love, inside this crazy place, she just couldn't do*

*it; she'd done everything to her best ability to*

*show them love and treat them with the up most respect; but her heart was gone just like their and she couldn't stay there anymore; so she left, caught up in this crazy city, with no love for anyone; she then realized she had fallen into Satan's trap and knew with a heart like hers she wouldn't be going back up!-**Tahisha Hamed***

## *At a loss of My Mother (4/16/2006)*

*Always knew who she was, and felt love for her;*

*though I was not raised under her eyes I always*

*held her close to my heart; sometimes I would cry*

*in the night as a child for I wanted her there, but*

*after a while I'd stop because I felt that was how it*

*was suppose to be but still  to me it wasn't fair;*

*Another woman was there to take care of me, I*

*appreciated what she'd done but still I couldn't see*

*the woman who gave birth to me; spoke a few*

*times and believe I've seen her more than twice;*

*I'm at a loss of My Mother*

*Now that she's with God I cannot cry for the pain*

*of her death, but I cry because I feel I didn't have*

*enough time to hold her, talk to her, be with her*

*and be seen right in her face; though I'm growing,*

*with her spirit near, my love for her can never and*

*will never disappear!!-**Tahisha Hamed***

### <u>6/08/2006</u>

*If I would've had a better understanding*

*I would've been a better person*

*I accept who I am and who I'm growing to*

*become*

*But I wish I could turn around and change*

*a few things*

*If I would have known of all the pain*

*I wouldn't have continued to go insane*

*Never wanted the negative, always wanting*

*the positive*

*NO LOVE, NO SEX, NO INTIMACY,*

*JUST A FRIEND TO HOLD ME*

*I've grown to learn a lot*

*Though it may not show*

*I KNOW EVERYTHING YOU TELL ME*

*I just keep it in closed doors*

*I wish the pain could go all away*

*BUT WE ALL*

*Have to learn from our mistakes-**Tahisha***

***Hamed***

### _Laying My Life Down (7/09/2006)_

_I have been asked to lay my life down_

_Before this man_

_To let go of all of my desires and treasures_

_So He can shine,_

_No to be seen in me_

_I did not question His request_

_Simply because I was already completing it_

_Though I pray for what He says to let go,_

_In my heart I feel that only He and I are_

_one,_

_But I'm not completely close with him_

_Because I'm still trying to get close to Him_

_My father,_

_My Lord and Savior_

_Laying my life down for you_

*Is no problem for me. –**Tahisha Hamed***

**08/12/2006**

I'm living in God's eyes but living with people

who aren't exactly with Him. Though they believe

in Him, I feel as though Satan is trying to bring as

much negativity in my presence as he possibly can.

**10/19/2006**

How do you know whether u fit in or not? Just

because people laugh and smile with you doesn't

mean you actually have a connection with them.

Not everyone is your friend, so why are you with

these people? Is it so you don't feel like a loner? Is

it because you hate being alone? Do you want

company? Life will drive you crazy. "I don't

know." "Don't know what?" "Who I really am,

whether I'm depressed, and if I need to go into

another space or area instead of where I've been?

I'm lost." I think to myself a lot. I'm lazy and just

don't know where I want to be right now. No one

can solve my "problems" whatever they may be. I

just know I really need someone to talk to, because

honestly I feel like I'm losing my mind.

Everything is so confusing to me. I'm really, truly,

lost and confused, maybe even depressed.

## 11/11/06

*I ask the Lord to take me away*

*When I'm feeling pain*

*I ask Him this because*

*I always go insane*

*When feeling pain*

*I feel pain when thinking*

*My mate is cheating*

*I feel pain when feeling alone*

*I feel pain when love in my heart*

*Isn't shown*

*I ask the Lord to take me away*

*When I'm feeling pain*

*At times I don't understand*

*Why I feel the way I do*

*I just know my heart is black*

*My soul is cold*

*And my spirit is nothing but stone*

*My clouds aren't blue and shiny*

*But they are grey and cloudy*

*At times I may pray about my feelings*

*But they appear never once again*

*I ask the lord to take me away*

*When I'm feeling pain*

*I always try to change how I feel*

*But the darkness in me*

*Is more than real*

**-Tahisha Hamed**

**12/4/2006**

God has shown me that I have two families, whom have filled the place of my mother and father.

**12/19/2006**

I never could accept the fact my birth mother wasn't here for me. I always felt as if I wasn't wanted. Even though I had someone who took care of me, it wasn't the same as having your birth mother there. I love my birth mother (Teresa) very much, but I never had the chance to live with her growing up. I did spend some time with her in my life before she passed. I was devastated and jealous. I was jealous because I felt my other brothers and sisters had the chance to spend more time with her than I did. I felt it wasn't fair but I grew out of it and accepted that she was in a better place. Every since her death in 2004 I was depressed, I became sad and/or very angry around 2005 and in 2006 I was very emotional. I began to stop showing my feelings and denying them because I no longer wanted to hurt. However, in the end I did hurt. I had to explain to a friend and their parent that I wanted to rest for a long time, but their parent explained to me that is not the way to go. I wanted to "rest" because my mother Teresa nor my father were there for me. Even when we do have that guardian or other parent, we still question and sometimes feel empty or alone. but no matter where I was or where I've been, I always felt alone. Yes I had the family I grew up knowing but eventually their love wasn't enough. I had questions I needed answered, but no one seemed to have the answer for me, simply because they couldn't relate to my situation. People will tell you they understand but they actually they don't because they haven't walked in your shoes.

**12/21/2006**

I always wanted to be with Teresa, but my father still did not want me to be with her. To this very day he doesn't know I've spent time with her. Sometimes during the night I would cry because I wanted her. I even prayed that God kept angels around her. He did for a long time but one night God had the angels carry her home. I wasn't ready for her to leave, but God knew the time, so I had to let it go.

# 2007-2008 Wobbling

# "trying to maintain

**01/01/2007**

Today is a brand new day for me. Today will be the day I renew myself with the Lord. Today I look towards the future and not the past. Today I become someone living for God and not myself or Satan. I want this day and this year to be more memorable than any past years. I become someone special today! I become someone important, I become someone who not only the Lord loves but I too love. I want to love my Lord and Savior, myself.

## 01/07/2007

I really enjoyed my day yesterday, even though

Friday night, I wasn't so happy or  yesterday

morning, but it had gotten better after I had prayed.

## 2/04/2007

Today is my first day going back to church. Ever

since I stopped going to church, I noticed not very

good things have been happening. I'd pray every

now and then and tell Jesus how hurt or mad I was.

Yet I still never accepted what I asked God to do

and He did.

## 8/18/2007

I haven't been praying and I know I need to stop

stalling. I have no reason to keep putting it off to

the side, but yet I am. I know my life won't get any

better unless I get into the word of God and pray. I

have no patience and I don't want to hear what

anyone has to tell me. I know that's not God's way and I know I need to do something like pray right now, right away, before my life gets worse. I don't want anything to happen to me. I need Jesus to help me so much. I'm no longer worried about love. I'm worried about God! I'm worried about being single, I'm not ready to mingle. I just want to do me and worry about what God wants for me to do for him. I have time to focus on working and going to school for my Lord and Savior. I don't want to be a failure in life. I want to make something better of myself. I don't want to be like anyone who let life sink them to the bottom of the bottle. Life is so much better than what people see. This life is not the end but God has given it to us, so we can make something better of it so we can do even better after this. And if I'm wrong then, hey, I know God will lead me the way he wants me to go and change to become the person He created me to be. I know God has my back so I'm not going to worry any longer.

**8/24/2007**

"Don't envy sinners, but always continue to fear the Lord; for surely you have a future ahead of you; your hope will not be disappointed." – Proverbs 23:17-18

Life at times can be really complicated, but it's up to us to get on our knees and pray to God about our situations. It's people like me who will go through so much pain & that's the only time I'll call on God. I don't want to do that. I know God can't be able to do what He wants to do with me if that's the only time I call on him. It's just so much more

that can be done with my life if I would just really

focus on God, you know? It's sad, because I have

to go through so much pain just to see that God is

the one who can do for me and provide me with all

the things I need in my life. Why can't I just come

to God through good times not just bad times, huh?

Why must I see the dark side before I come to the

light? I have gone through the same thing these

last 2-3 relationships, giving myself to God then

stopping because some guy distracted me. A few

people have told me that I'm going to be a great

person chosen by Christ because I've gone through

so much and yet I still, at times don't see what they

see! I have lived life trying to make others happy

and even right now today I still don't do what

makes Tahisha happy. Why? I don't know maybe I'm scared, I don't know. I just wish it could be God and me. He's just shaking me telling me to wake up because I don't have long. I want to be with Christ when I die. I want to be at peace. I want to be the person God wants me to be!!! Life is getting better and better every day when I just think and talk about God. I know he has my back and that's the only reason I feel safe going home at night!!

## August 25, 2007

Patience is evidence of the Holy Spirit working in our lives. (Galatians 5:22) "But when the Holy Spirit controls our lives, he will produce this kind of fruit in us; love, joy, peace, patience, kindness, goodness, faithfulness." I write scriptures everyday feeling like someone might need them but then when I look back I see that I'm the one who needs it. The scripture I wrote above I feel is really for me because I know I need some patience in my life because it is so low. I can't stand waiting on somebody to do something. I get irritated really fast and just get mad, and reading that verse lets me know, the Holy Spirit is not working in my life.

**September 10, 2007**
A lot has happened since I moved out the house I grew up in and I don't regret leaving but I do wonder what would've happened if I would've stayed home. But then I tell myself not to think like that because I wouldn't have had this learning experience. I learned a lot within these last 3 months, and am still learning. I've done some

things to hurt people and they've done some things to hurt me but never again will I live with another person. I want my own space and I know it will take time to do that since I'm in school now but it's okay I'll make sure I do it.

**<u>September 19, 2007</u>**
Sometimes we make decisions whether they be small or huge that make us feel low or high. But in the end we still feel like crying, especially when in debt. Being in debt can make you want to cry, scream and maybe even want to give up. You miss days of going to work either because you can't get there or get home, but you can't, all you can do is wait on God.

*"Sometimes experience is the best teacher for life*

*lessons*

*Sometimes it just takes some good advice*

*To understand a simple session*

*Sometimes we get caught up in our own confusion*

*To recognize a serious blessing"-* **Tahisha Hamed**

## December 28, 2007

How do you know when your completing God's will in your life? For weeks I have been happy and thankful, now after the week of Christmas, my energy seems low. I'm not reading and studying my Bible and my flesh, I say my flesh, is yearning for male comfort. I just need to let it go. I want to be a dedicated Christ follower, I don't want to just be the one who starts reading my Bible, starts praying and praising and then when I want what I used to have, I stop. I want to be able to just pray through everything I ever go through. The Lord is my father, He is my everything so I want to & need to turn to Him when I'm going through anything.

**January 1, 2008**

My dear Heavenly Father, I am trying to do right.

Lord I am trying to obey but God the old me is

trying to overcome, so Father I just come to you

now and ask for your forgiveness; Lord I don't

want to become a backslider like before. Jesus I

need your help Lord. I need you by my side day

and night Jesus. Please Father, please Lord, I really

want to do right, I really want to live a Godly life.

Lord please Jesus please protect me from all harm

and evil. I know I must obey your laws and

commands. So Jesus I'm willing to do all Lord, all

the things that I have to do to live an eternal life

with you. I love you God; I really do love you

Jesus; please God please don't give up on me!!!

*I Corinthians 1: 8-9*

*God will keep you Strong,*

*God does what he says he'll do*

**2/18/2008**

I honestly love the Lord and the life he has blessed me to wake up to everyday. Though I may not have a car or my own apartment/house, God still blesses me to get to school, church, work, and back home safely. Today I stayed home in the bed and just read my Bible. I then began reading over my past journal entries and they made me extremely happy because God has brought me through a lot. Not just sex, but heartache from myself as well as from others, as well as bad nerves. I really love God for all he has done for little ole me.

## 2/27/2008

I started good with God in the beginning of this year, I prayed for a good church home and a good pastor. God answered my prayers just at the right time. Now that two months are about to be over, I've realized I started seeking people for answers I should've gotten from God. Don't get me wrong I love my church family, but I have moved away from God on a prayer-faith based relationship. I have noticed that I have received the Holy Spirit. It's not the same as before. Where I would get excited deep down in my stomach, now I feel as though I'm forcing it to come out. Honestly, I feel as though I really need to examine myself. Where is my faith level with God? Where & how does God see me? Am I a hypocrite or am I a true worshipper for God, but have been seeking people more than Christ? That may just exactly what's happened. I know I love God, but I've started speaking out to people and have not been quiet for the spirit of God. I miss really telling the Lord I truly love him. Not because the pastor tells me to say it but because I see the church members doing it. I want it to be from within. What has been happening in this life God has blessed me to have every day but yet I take it for granted. Yes I can wake up every day, pray, say, "thank you God for allowing me to see another day," and read my bible. But what happened to witnessing and trying to invite more people to church? What happened to my passion for God?

**2/27/08**

The day before Sunday December 2<sup>nd</sup>, 2007, my path was on its way to a burning hell. I was doing what I wanted but because of the Lord Almighty's gracious love for me, I have survived. God kept me from being molested, raped and killed December 1<sup>st</sup>, 2007. God has really showered His protecting arms around me. God has just been wonderful to me. All I have to do is just really believe in Him, live a God-fearing life and help bring others who were on my path to Him. Man I love God! He has truly blessed me and brought me through some really tough trials but because of who He is, He has given me another chance.

## 6/5/2008

Last week I was filled with joy. I was witnessing to people and the Lord was the only thing on my mind. This week has been different. I have prayed but my anger didn't seem to go anywhere but rise higher. I know it's not because of companionship, because that doesn't even play a part in my life anymore!!! So far I know guys are not part of my anger. Sometimes I just wish I could leave, you know? (Writing like I'm talking to somebody-crazy!!!). But I do want to just get away, somewhere by a beach or marina and just watch the sun set, while the sky turns into those beautiful pink, red, and blue colors. That sets my mind and soul free. Just standing there watching the clouds move across the sky; that's peace to me. Right now at this very moment I feel like crying. Why? I

don't know what to do.

**6/12/08**

I'm lying down in the living room (my room)

thinking- God has brought me through so much.

Not just the fact of almost being raped, but through

being broke and depressed. I didn't forget about

everything I was going through 10mos ago. Even

though its more I experienced before those ten

months, I thank God for rescuing me from hell;

Even though this very moment I'm not as joyful or

thankful as I should be, I thank God that he really

did have mercy on my life!! God has brought me

through so much pain, heartache, depression, and

just losing my sanity. God is not just a spirit, GOD

IS REAL!!! He is not just my Savior, my Father,

or any other name the Bible mentions!! Even

though I may not know all God is in the Bible, He

is more to me than just what the world and Bible says. God really is my everything and I can say right now, I am not happy with myself. I want but in all honesty, God is keeping me from falling all over again. God has really had mercy on me and as much as I was thanking him when I had nothing and was really struggling, my praise is not the same. God has really blessed and showered his love down on me. I thank God for truly having patience and mercy on me because I was on my way straight to death.

*Life is really funny but you're not to take it as a joke!!!- Tahisha Hamed*

### 7/11/08

I am always in a situation where history keeps

repeating itself. I am always running through the

rough roads in my life and I never stop to really

pray. I never really talk to God because I'm

ashamed of the things I've done, So I run and hide

from his Word because I know my spirit is going

to be convicted. I become afraid because I know

I've done wrong, but also because my world flesh

having ways don't want to change and live the way

God wants me to. I become scared to live for God

because I still want to be held by a young man and

enjoy his company and the affection he gives me. I

know God will give that to me when the time is

right but I just want it to be on my own time to be

honest.

When I'm visiting my best friend, I realize I'm myself. I'm not covering myself because I'm ashamed of what I've done but I can cry to my best friend about what I've done and be comforted whereas anywhere else—I'm ashamed and afraid of people judging me. I'm tired of living life the way others want me too. Yes, I'll take advice from other people but I refuse to allow another human being take control of my life. I just want to be myself, NO MATTER WHERE I AM!!!

## *Trying Not To Give Up*

### *(07/23/2008)*

*School, God, Work, Work, School*

*Work, Work, School, God, God*

*God, School, God, School, Work*

*I am trying not to give up on school!*

*I am trying not to give up on God!*

*I am trying not to give up on Work!*

*How does one maintain the right way of living,*

*when there were no real positive role models?*

*How does one continue to move forward in*

*personal goals if elders never taught you how?*

*How does one make it through college alone?*

*How does one love God and walk with God*

*without faith alone?*

*How does one learn to love themselves?*

*How does one learn to have standards if none*

*were ever taught?*

*How does one live life to the fullest knowing the*

*spiritual war is happening and all that you have*

*now and ever accomplished will disappear like the*

*wind?*

*How does one maintain trying not to give up on*

*life?*

*Every day I have woken up with all kinds of*

*worries, troubles, punishment, happiness and fear.*

*I have questioned everyday asking, "is this my last*

*day?" or "when will it all end?"*

*I have wondered, why have I not taken school*

*serious?*

*I have questioned the people who are a part of my*

*life- "why are you here?"*

*I have looked at myself in the mirror and seemed*

*disgusted!!*

*I have questioned who I really am?*

*Am I a child of God?*

*Am I a disciple, a witness for Christ?*

*WHO AM I??*

*Who is this young lady who wakes up and feels*

*nothing in her heart?*

*Who is this lady who works to pay her small bills*

*to have a roof over her head?*

*Who is that girl who goes to school but loses*

*focus?*

*WHO AM I?*

*What is my life's purpose?*

*Why must I question the life I live?*

*Why must I wonder if ill continue to live?*

51

*What is life truly about?*

*"Praising God and living a God fearing life and*

*trying to be like Christ?"*

*What is a purpose driven life?*

*What is praising God?*

*How does one Love love God?*

*How does one continue to ask for forgiveness and*

*yet your committing the same sin over and over?*

*How does one let go of the past to live for the*

*future?*

*WHO ARE YOU?*

*WHO AM I?*

*WHO ARE THE PEOPLE WHO WALK THIS*

*EARTH?*

*How does one find the real meaning of living a*

*Godly life?*

*"The Holy Bible"*

*How do you and I, as children of God, not sin?*

*How? How? How?*

**-*Tahisha Hamed***

# "Struggling to Walk"

**7/30/08**

Bible Study Notes- New Ark Baptist Church-

Pastor Darnell Manuel

Back II the Basics

<u>Pray-</u> NO COMMUNICATION WITH GOD= NO RESPONSE

- Kneeling= show reverence to God

- God cannot honor your prayer because your not sincere & you have no effort

- The Word is your sword- your weapon

- As a leader in the ministry in the church, your suppose to be on point with God and your pastor- you have to study your word and pray

- Emotional people- no help, only happy

- Spirit filled people- get helped and receive the Word in your heart

- What difference will it make to have everything in life & lose your soul?

    1. Attitude has to change

    2. Desire- what is it?

        - Desire has to change

        - No Life = No Praise

    3. Mentality has to change

        - Church + God = One (?)

- Need a "God First" Mentality

- Pay Tithes & Offerings- God looks out for those who give tithes and offerings

- Attitude+ Mentality+ Desire: ALL NEEDS TO CHANGE

- Church is NOT the place to always bring your mess (?)

- Don't complain when you get corrected

- If you really want to get BETTER and have a DESIRE to CHANGE, then YOU WILL.

## 7/31/2008

I have learned to realize my life is falling into pieces- ha-ha. I knew it was falling into pieces when I started living life the way I wanted to and not the way God wanted me to. I learned my life is the way it is because I made it this way. No one is the cause of my problems but me. I can't get any financial aid because of my G.P.A. This is my fault, because I decided to put work before school and now my relationship with God is my fault & affected badly because I put work before God. So now, my financial status is not the way I would like for it to be, nor is my schooling but yet it's my fault because I pulled away from God.

**8/3/2008**
*Smile!! You've made it farther from where you were this time last year*

**8/4/2008**
Okay, so I went to service yesterday and it was

great. I let go of my issues and actually

surrendered. I told my pastor I was scared to

live for Christ & he cut me off & said I have a

lot of emotions built up and that's okay (??). I

really did not want to go up to the sanctuary but

obedience was the calling, so I did what was

right and let my pastor pray for me!!! I'm

happy I let go.

## 8/8/2008

This time last year, I was a mess. I was depressed and felt alone. I had no one to talk to that was willing to listen to what I had to say. Now, I'm a changed person. I no longer put others before God or myself. I have learned that I have to make sacrifices that either will not make me happy or whoever I have to sacrifice with or for will not be happy. God has brought me through a lot, not just last year but my whole life. He has taught and showed me the rights and the wrongs that I wasn't willing to learn from anyone else. He brought me from heartache, disappointment, shame and so much more. I do want to be a strong mighty young woman of Christ. And I know I could've been one but I was afraid… afraid of being alone again and pushed out feeling like an outcast but now I don't care.

*Sometimes being alone is the best time to find out who you really are and what you want in life!!! –Tahisha Hamed*

Being alone helps you find a peace of mind with no radio or television or cell phone on, you can find out so much about yourself. Life does involve love between family, friends and your very own partner, but life is really about finding out who God is and living a God-fearing life, while also trying to find out who you are yourself. How can you find out who you are if you're always around people, and always have a cluttered mind. Life is so much more than what we as human beings make it out to be.

God is the only answer to our problems. He is

the only one that determines the time & day we

shall die. God is the Father, the one who will

punish us when we do the wrong. God is,

should be and always will be, my everything;

because I know I NEVER WOULD'VE MADE

IT this far, this new year (2008), without

Him!!!

**8/9/2008**

I feel like crying right now. I want my own place, I want to go to school full time, and I want to work. But my future from now shows me I can't. I know God will make a way; I just have to trust and believe that this trail won't last forever. This test of faith is only temporary and I know I can make it through this. I just have to believe in God. I really want to cry right now but I'm not, because I know I'm stronger than this and I know God will help me get through this. Life is about trying- trying to make it to Heaven, trying to make it through school, trying to just make it through life period. Sometimes we will fail but that's only to make us stronger, for now & when something similar or tougher comes our way. I know I can and will make it through this. I will encourage myself and believe God is walking with me. I just have to hold my head up, smile, and say, "God is on my side and he will never let me go."

**8/10/08**

New Ark Baptist Church: "From Private Pain to

Public Praise"

**1 Samuel 1**: <u>Private Praise</u>

- Stop thinking about what others think

  about you.

- God wants to deliver you from your pain

  today!!

- Leave your pain with God and walk with

  praise.

Hannah- barren

- Unable to have children

- Mother of Samuel

- Had to deal with the other wife who

  provoked her

When you have a void, IT WILL ALWAYS BE THERE!! (???)

She went to the right place at the right time and talked to the right person

Peace- be calm

You came barren but you ought to leave with a harvest.

Samuel- name of God

**1 Samuel 2:** <u>Public Praise</u>

<u>**8/10/2008**</u>

New Ark Baptist Church- Women's Day Program

Lady Richardson- "Transformation; It's a mind thing"

1. Take responsibility of your thoughts and mind.

- You got to have the holy spirit of God to have change

- New= never existed before

- It's not all the responsibility, you have to cooperate

- New mind + New Change = New life

- You have to be consistent

  1. The bible

     - Open it

     - Read it

     - Meditate on it

- **Psalms 119:11** *"your word I have hidden in my heart, that I might not sin against You"*

- **Phil. 4:9** *"The things which you learned and received and heard and saw in me, these do, and the God of peace will be with you"*

2. Agree with God's way of doing things

- **Amos 3:3** *"Can two walk together, unless they are agreed?"*
- Accept our way of thinking is wrong if it's not God's way
- Walk by Faith, not by Sight!!

3. Decide to meditate on the word of God.

- Tell your mind to be quiet because Satan will try to plant things in your mind.
-

**8/15/2008**
Dear Lord,

I know I have turned away from you, because I wanted to fulfill my own desires. God, you know all the things I have done, thought, and wanted to do. Lord, I am sorry!!! I'm sorry for saying all the ungodly things I have done. I'm sorry for treating everyone unkindly. Lord, I'm sorry for walking away from you. Lord, you have protected me from a lot of danger during the times I have rode the bus late at night, when I've walked alone at night; lord, you are my every thing. Lord, I just say thank you. Thank you for giving me chance after chance when you didn't have to. Lord, you could have destroyed me, while in my sin but Lord; you had mercy on me and gave me another chance.

Lord, I thank you. All the times after my sin,

I'd go to sleep wondering will this be my last

day but God you keep having mercy on me, and

Lord I don't deserve it. God, I just thank you

for all the things you're doing and you've done.

Lord, I pray Jesus, for the strength to walk for

you. Lord, I pray for the strength to witness to

more people to be saved. Lord, please God, just

discipline me lord to become the young lady

you need me to be. God, please Jesus, please

just allow me to really get to know you, and

have a strong faith to walk & believe you are

the way for anything in my life, to be possible

to go forth. God, I do love you, I just become

afraid to do right according to your Word, but

God I'm surrendering and I'm going to do what's right. Thank You.

## 9/6/2008

I can't keep failing the test!!! I can't keep beginning the full walk with God and sin again. I know I really want to be God fearing woman and truly dedicated to Him but I'm not and I wish I was. Yes, I know people make many mistakes but sometimes it's not a mistake; it's really you wanting to fulfill your own desires. How many times can you tell God, "I'm sorry." until He says "enough is enough" and He'll let Satan just have you? How many times... I'm not going to say or tell God, I'm sorry and still fulfill my desires. I'm going to actually move forward with the whole situation and just keep pushing to being on the level God wants me to be on. Yes, I want more of my desires, but it's not worth losing God's mercy and forgiveness.

I know God has a real plan for me to pass every

test that comes my way, so if that means I have

to sit in the house everyday and just force

myself to read the Bible, I will!!

## 9/07/2008

I make and have made many mistakes in my life, but I have decided that when God tests me, I will be ready. Meaning- I will read my word, I will stop indulging in sinful activities and I will first and foremost, put God as my main focus. Yes that did seem hard to understand and do, but when God is included in every activity in my life, it's easy. I know, I love God and I know I want to go to Heaven, so I have to live everyday of my life doing what I need to do to please him and get to Heaven. Maybe Mrs. Manuel was right, maybe I don't know the full meaning of being saved, but I do know something- I will always have God and no matter what other people may say or think, God is always in my heart. God knows, he knows a

lot about me; He knows I make mistakes.

### 9/12/2008

So yesterday, I had a real scary, yet shocking spiritual experience with God. My body felt like it was taken over by someone else. I was in the house alone and I started talking to God (and myself) aloud. Asking Him if I was going to hell because I'm a sinner? And even though it seemed like someone else was in me, I now feel good. I really pray I don't have split personalities and that I'm not bipolar, but today I feel really good. At first I woke up feeling the same, negative way as yesterday, but now I feel excellent. I know God is still looking out for me. I know He smiles and cries for me. I don't know what God sees but I know that whenever I'm asleep or awake, God is watching my back.

I know that when I feel alone at night, God wraps His arms around me. Maybe yesterday's experience was part of my breakthrough. I know there are many more to come, but as I reflect on that experience with God, I see now and feel in my heart, that was my time to clean my mind, body and spirit. God loves me- yes He does!! And I know that he sees me trying to do what I can to live right.

**9/14/2008**
Dear Lord,

I don't know nor do I understand why I have anger towards a few members of the church. Today God, as you have seen, my mind was saying negative things towards the pastor, then I slightly flashed on two deacons. Lord, please help me God, to understand why I am angry. Lord Please just get me to really understand why it's like this. My mind doesn't seem to be at peace nor does my spirit, so God please just open up my heart and mind God so I can stop feeling this way. Lord, I really don't get it Jesus, I don't. I don't know if I need counseling or even if I need prayer but God just help me. PLEASE LORD, JUST HELP ME.

## 09/15/2008

So, today during school, I signed up for counseling. I was just lying down on one of the couches at school and it came over me that I really need someone to talk to about what I'm feeling inside. Yes, I am praying and talking to God about what I'm facing, but I feel that I need to release this pain more to another person. I'm not saying that God can't heal me from what I'm dealing with; I just need to work more on my faith. If my faith level was stronger, I may not have gone to the counselor's office; but then again, I don't know what God's plan and desire of my life is. I can only take it one step at a time and believe that I can be and will be a successful happy-joy filled young woman of God. I know when and if I

really go see the counselor on Thursday I will

be afraid, just like I am now. I love God, I

know deep down inside I love Him. I just want

to be able to show Him in all the things I do.

## 10/27/2008

Even though, my mom was not there to give me the love from a mother I wanted, I understand that it was the way God planned it. I understand that I would not be who I am now, had things been different. I cry because I felt I deserved and had the right to know her and be with her and be with and around her. I cry because she will never be at any of the special events in my life. I cry because I will never wake up and am able to walk into the next room to hug her, sleep next to her, cry to her about some guy who hurt me. I will never know what it's like to get in trouble or make her mad. I'll never know and that hurts. The fact I'm 19 years old and I'll never see my mother's face again. I'll never hear her say she loves me. NEVER! NEVER!

NEVER! I always dreamed to just live with her,

to love her, to care for her; I always dreamed of

that. But yet it was just a dream. Not reality,

just a dream that will never come true. She's

gone and she'll never come back. I can cry for

her and I can scream to God, saying, "she was

supposed to stay and love me." But it will not

change anything. Yeah, I might heal from it and

be able to continue walking through life,

pushing to accomplish my goals; but I'll have

to move forward and tell myself "though my

mother may not be here to love and watch me

grow, I know she loved me." I want to be able

to move on with my life. Yes, I will hold what

memories I have of her, in my heart and when I

become a mother, I will share the goodness I

received from my mother with them.

## 12/08/2008

Life is beautiful. Life is great. People are unique, different, good and evil but God, God is magnificent. He changes the weather, direct your path in life, blesses you and punishes you but God is greater because He loves you and he forgives you for your sins but He does have patience which runs out.

I have made many choices where God should have really stopped my very existence but He didn't. He kept pushing me to do better.

## 12/14/2008

*"Only a fool despises a parent's discipline.*
*Whoever learns from correction is wise"*
*Proverbs 15:5*

Whoever learns from correction is wise...

wise? Correction? Well I have learned a lot from myself as well as others. I have learned that God is above any priority you have. I have learned that you must plan/write out your goals and give yourself a time length because you'll only procrastinate when you don't. I have learned not to let my past dictate my future. I have learned to let negative things go. I learned that when you think positive, in return you'll receive positivity. I could go on and on about all I have learned in the past two years BUT I'm not. I'm going to take all I have learned, gained, and lost with me. The New Year for me means "STEPPING OUT ON FAITH"…

### _Shutting Down (12/25/08)_

_Closed mouth, closed eyes_

_Feeling anger & confusion on the inside_

_Yelling, stomping, reacting to these_

_circumstances_

_Wondering why?_

_Why am I facing this?_

_Why must I place myself in these situations?_

_Afraid, maybe even_

_Even if this is where I wanna be._

_Questions, yet no answers_

_I'm shutting down_

_I'm in my zone_

_See, hear_

_No one but myself_

_Digging deep down_

*Thinking of what?*

*What I see for me*

*Wait, I'm tuned out*

*No one is listening 2 me*

*I can't hear myself speak*

*I've been shut out by the crowd!!!*

**-Tahisha Hamed**

### *Gurl Shout (12/25/08)*

*Scream and shout*

*Let that pain out*

*Praise his holy name*

*Gurl don't be ashamed*

*Live right*

*Stop acting a fool*

*The world is evil*

*But Jesus is cool!*

*Gurl shout!!*

*Let that anger out!*

*He uniquely shaped you*

*4 his purpose*

*Understand*

*You're temporarily standing*

*On this world's surface*

*God's love is permanent*

*But this pleasure is not*

*You're hurting on the inside*

*Cuz you're not lukewarm*

*You're hot.*

*Gurl shout!!*

*Let that praise out*

*Your blessing is on the way*

*So take this 1$^{st}$ step*

*And let god guide you everyday.*

**-Tahisha Hamed**

## *<u>Take Me Away!!(12/25/08)</u>*

*Take me away*

*Take me to a much*

*Higher place*

*Take my mind*

*Take my mind out*

*Out of this "state"*

*Take the feeling of unhappiness*

*Release from me*

*Allow me to see,*

*See the beauty of life*

**-Tahisha Hamed**

# THE END!

**P.S.  THIS IS ONLY THE BEGINNING**

"Be strong and of good courage, do not fear nor
be afraid of them; for the Lord your God, He *is*
the One who goes with you. He will not leave
you nor forsake you."
**Deuteronomy 31:6**

## The Journey Continues…

## "5743 Gaskill Street" 2011

How in the world did I end up here? Unable to breathe, move, encourage or even have belief. This once was a happy place for me but now all I feel is heaviness, doubt, fear, and confusion. Oh, I know where it's coming from, yet so many trials & tests have come my way in these three years, how can I possibly find God here? How can God hear me? I've been calling on him, yet this last year seems as though God is so far from me. Pray? I do that. Read His Word? I do that too; yet I'm not hearing from God.

Lord on the inside, I feel horrible. Ugh!!! Why lord? Why Lord? Are you hearing me? Are you listening to me? Ugh!!! I'm hurt. I'm angry

Lord!!! How can one go from living a decent

successful life; attending college, grades are great,

stable finances, bills paid, not just on time but also

early!!! God how did we end up here? How Lord?

I was content. I was peaceful. Just in the same way

you've allowed people to be a blessing to me, by

providing shelter, I've done the same. Helped so

many people and yet I'm down to nothing but a

studio/garage apartment. Rodents Lord!!!

Rodents!!! Trying to maintain my peace of mind

Lord!!! Come on God, I need you. Please come

through. I cannot do this without you.

Lord, we use to be so close. Where have you gone?

Lord, you've said you'll "never leave me or

forsake me." God please, you see the tears in my

eyes, and you feel the pain in my heart. Am I no

longer your child? GOD!!! GOD!!! GOD!!! HELP ME!!! You see I'm calling out to you. I'm on begging knees Lord!! UGH!!!

How father? How did I loose sight of the ultimate prize? You know, the one of me and you just living happily ever after. Ha Ha right! A fairytale; that I could possibly live peacefully and have a content life with Christ. My God, what in Heavens am I doing wrong??? Ahh, let's see. I now drink a lot; yeah guess I'm an alcoholic. No one really knows though. No one sees how I drown my sorrows in the bottle. Doing this in-home care, watching these patients die off slowly and it's just adding to my sadness. Losing the patience I once had to care for these people. Feeling lost and hopeless.

The young man I loved, ugh!!! We'll he's gone

just like everyone else in my life. Why cant I see

what happened to me was just wrong? Why am I in

denial? Why am I even still here? I mean yes, the

Bay Area will always be home, but I want to see

something different. Surprising the only thing I do

believe in is that it's time for me to leave this

place.

Los Angeles has been calling my name since I was

a child; yet I'm still living life for everyone else.

Let's be honest Lord, all I want to do is write

poems, books, Hallmark cards, while living in a

nice home in Los Angeles. Who knows maybe I'll

one day write movies with Steven Spielberg. I

know I have big dreams and so many people

including myself have found ways to tell me "you

can't make any money doing that. Get a career." I mean when will I just start living for myself? Damien Davis asked me to go to Los Angeles with him and Lord, as bad as I wanted to just run away with him and finally see what you have out there for me… I missed my ticket. Stayed right here and now look at me; no money, grades are terrible and rent is way past due!!!

Can't keep a stable relationship with anyone; Not family, friends, co-workers, church members, I mean nobody Lord! Why did this have to happen to me? I mean do you really just not want me? Yes, granted Lord, you have truly been here for me; oh but God where are you now? I know I keep asking but God, I've never felt you so far away. We had the best relationship God. How did we lose it? I mean God, my thoughts are not at all positive; you know you see all things.

What happened between 2009 and now (2011)? Was it my last relationship? Was I too focused on what turned out to be temporary? How could I just be so foolish? Someone needs to come help me. Lord, think I'm going crazy!! Maybe I should go see a therapist. Yeah, go talk to someone's about all this pain.

You know Lord; I keep replaying how he and I ended. Ugh!! I wish I could erase all the memories of him and me. I hate... okay no I hate him. God I know that's not nice to say, but was he nice to me? He mentally and emotionally neglected me. Yea I admit, I was/am very emotional. Maybe if I were heartless, it would have been better. Maybe we should have just given up a long time ago before this tragic encounter. How can one sit there and start talking/planning a life together and even try to bring a life into this world; just to wake up one day and can't even say hello. How father? So many tears shed so many empty promises…its ok… I guess… Guess he's not the one for me; guess this was another useless relationship that brought me nothing but pain. Ugh!! I dislike him so much. Jerk!!

God, can you just help me please? Rid me of all this anger and hatred. Bring me back to that place of peace. Everyone is saying how much I've changed but they don't know about this secret eating away at me. Oh no, no, no, I dare not speak of this pain brought on by everyone's favorite person!! How dare I? HOW DARE I NOT!?!?! I

really don't like these church members, him, and

anyone!!! I hate them all Lord!!!

I'm hurt Lord!!! How is it you'll show people

certain things but you won't show them this

father? Show them this pain. Ugh!!! No one is

listening to me, no one!!! In this hell hole all alone,

no more friends, no more "parties". It's all come to

an end. All of it. Life, life is just too much to

manage. Maybe, maybe one day everything will

get better. Maybe one day I'll love again, trust

again, and believe again. But today, life is just too

much to manage.

It's time to go. It's time to leave this place and find

somewhere new to go. Somewhere, where the

sounds of the sea bring me peace!! Somewhere,

where the sun shines bright in my life!! I need to find somewhere that my past doesn't follow. A new start!! A new journey!!! A new life!!! Somewhere my pain no longer is in control of me. I know I have a long way before getting to that heavenly place, but here on earth, you have a special place for me to have joy, peace, love, contentment, and faith!!! Yet, I wonder if I'll ever find that place…

To: God

From: A Broken Soul

www.ingramcontent.com/pod-product-compliance
Lightning Source LLC
Chambersburg PA
CBHW072012170626
46813CB00005B/2134